Merry Christmas
Chanelle,
from Gabrielle & Holly
with love & hugs
2009

The Perfect Christmas Gift

This book belongs to:

Princess *Chanelle*

The
gigi, God's Little Princess™
series includes:

gigi, God's Little Princess
in book and DVD formats

The Royal Tea Party

The Perfect Christmas Gift

And just for boys:
will, God's Mighty Warrior

gigi

God's Little Princess™

The Perfect Christmas Gift

Sheila Walsh

Illustrated by Meredith Johnson

Tommy NELSON®

A Division of Thomas Nelson Publishers
Since 1798

www.thomasnelson.com

GIGI, GOD'S LITTLE PRINCESS™: THE PERFECT CHRISTMAS GIFT

Text © 2006 by Sheila Walsh

Illustrations © 2006 by Tommy Nelson®, a Division of Thomas Nelson, Inc.

All rights reserved. No portion of this book may be reproduced in any form without the written permission of the publisher, with the exception of brief excerpts in reviews.

Published in Nashville, Tennessee, by Tommy Nelson®, a Division of Thomas Nelson, Inc.

Scripture quoted from the *International Children's Bible*®, *New Century Version*®, copyright © 1986, 1988, 1999 by Tommy Nelson®, a Division of Thomas Nelson, Inc., Nashville, Tennessee 37214.

Tommy Nelson® books may be purchased in bulk for educational, business, fundraising, or sales promotional use. For information, please email SpecialMarkets@ThomasNelson.com.

ISBN-10: 1-4003-0801-1
ISBN-13: 978-1-4003-0801-9

Printed in the United States of America
06 07 08 09 10 WRZ 5 4 3 2 1

This book is
dedicated with love
to Princess Annie,
our Nashville Gigi.

Gigi decided that if Christmas Day were December 26th instead of the 25th, she would probably explode!

"How many more days now, Daddy?" she asked at breakfast, teasing Lord Fluffy with a piece of bacon.

"Five more days, princess," her dad replied.

"Five more days?!" she cried. "Five more days . . . I'll never make it!"

Gigi's mother smiled. "I seem to remember that you felt that way last year and the year before that and the year before that."

"That was when I was a little kid, Mommy. Now I'm ready to begin my royal rule as God's little princess."

"Well, why don't you go upstairs and brush your *royal* hair before Frances gets here."

"Come, Lord Fluffy," Gigi said. "We shall retire to our chambers."

For as long as she could remember, Gigi had known she was of royal birth. Why else would her father call her *princess* as he kissed her goodnight? Daddies don't make things up!

"You may approach me," Gigi said, imagining her subjects lined up with arms full of gifts.

"How lovely!" she gushed, accepting a gold bracelet offered by a young girl.

"Perfume, how perfect!" she cried as an elderly gentleman knelt before her.

"Arise, sir," she offered graciously. "I'm sure your knees are hurting by now." It was important to Gigi that she rule with royal kindness.

"What *are* you up to now?" a voice asked from the doorway. It was Frances, Gigi's best friend. Frances was also a princess, and Gigi was quite certain that Frances didn't have her crown yet either.

"Frances, can you believe that it is still five days till Christmas?" Gigi said. "How will we survive?"

"It'll be tough," Frances agreed.
"We'll just take it one day at a time."

"I know!" Gigi cried.

"Let's dress up Lord Fluffy as the Baby Jesus to pass the time.
He'll love it!"

But Lord Fluffy seemed reluctant to *love* it.

That night after Frances had gone home, Gigi sat by the Christmas tree gazing up at the twinkling lights and the silver star at the very top.

"Let this be the year," she whispered. "I know I am ready to receive my royal crown. It's not easy to feel like a royal princess without a royal tiara with royal jewels."

"Can I interest anyone in some hot chocolate with marshmallows?" Gigi's daddy offered, as he sat a tray by the fireplace.

"Just one clue, Daddy? That's all—one clue. I'll take a *little* clue, a clue so tiny even a doctor or a library person wouldn't be able to guess," she begged.

"What do you think?" Gigi's daddy asked, as he passed a mug to her mom. "Shall we give her a little clue about her big present?"

"Let's see . . . it's something you have wanted for a while," Mommy began.

"It's white," Daddy added. "White with a touch of pink."

"Oh, my goodness! May I please be excused?"
Gigi asked in a hushed excitement.
"I have a royal call to make."

"Frances, I have the most amazing news!" she cried.
"Are you ready?"

"I think I am," Frances replied. "But sometimes with you, Gigi,
I think I am and discover that I most definitely am not."

"Frances . . . I know what my royal tiara looks like," Gigi said
with a squeal.

"I thought you wanted a crown," Frances asked.

"Details, details!" Gigi replied. "It's the same thing."

 "So, how did you find out, Gigi?"

"Well, I asked for a little clue that even really smart grownups wouldn't get . . . but I got it. It was pure, royal instinct!"

"So, what was the clue?" Frances asked.

"White and pink," Gigi said. "My crown has white diamonds with a big pink feather on the top!"

"Hmm, that's . . . that's . . . well, that's *unusual*," Frances said. "Did they say diamonds?"

"Not exactly . . . but that's what they meant," Gigi said with certainty. "One knows these things. Now I must wait like a proper princess."

Days dragged past. . . .

Finally, it was December 24th, Christmas Eve.

Gigi's daddy read stories about Baby Jesus—how He was born where animals are kept and how wise men from the East came to see Him.

"You would think that a *royal* baby would get a better bed than an animal feeding box," Gigi observed. "But at least He got gifts from the three wise men. That must have made Him feel royal."

"He *was* the gift," her daddy answered. "God's perfect present to all of us. Now go to sleep, princess."

Gigi woke up as the sun began to sparkle on the snow.
"It's Christmas! It's Christmas!" she cried, twirling Lord
Fluffy in the air. "Let's go, Fluff-Puff. You don't want to
miss my crowning."

"Oh, my goodness!" Gigi said, looking at the array of gifts around the tree. Her eyes surveyed the presents, looking for one that was crown-sized. She began to open them one by one.

"Aren't you going to open that big one?" her mommy asked.

"Not yet, Mommy," Gigi answered. She opened box after box, but there was no crown.

A large tear formed and rolled down her cheek.

"Gigi," her daddy said, "I think you should open that big box before it explodes!"

Gigi stared at the box and realized that it was moving. Crawling over to it, she peeked inside.

Two tiny eyes stared back at Gigi. She threw off the lid, and there, inside, was the most darling, white, little puppy with a white collar covered in princess-pink jewels.

"It's a poodle!"
Gigi said in amazement.

Gigi thought for a moment. She looked into the puppy's big eyes, then announced in her most royal voice:

"I shall call her . . . Tiara! She is a royally perfect Christmas gift!"

That night, Gigi lay in bed with a soft, white bundle beside her and a larger white bundle muttering cat-threats from under the bed.

"I guess when the shepherds saw Jesus in a box of hay, they got a big surprise too," she said.

"I'm sure they did, Gigi," her daddy replied. "Who would have ever thought that the very best gift in the world would come in such an unexpected package? Goodnight, princess."

"Goodnight, Daddy," Gigi said. "Thank you so much for Tiara. My royal court is growing."

As Gigi's eyes began to close, she said to her two royal pets, "Just wait till I tell Frances that what *I thought* was my crown barks and has to go outside every two hours!"

"But perhaps the *real* royal crown—that is, the one that goes on my head—could come on my birthday?"

The angel said to them, "Don't be afraid, because I am bringing you some good news. It will be a joy to all the people. Today your Savior was born in David's town. He is Christ, the Lord. This is how you will know him: You will find a baby wrapped in cloths and lying in a feeding box."

Luke 2:10-12

When the wise men saw the star, they were filled with joy. They went to the house where the child was and saw him with his mother, Mary. . . . They gave him treasures of gold, frankincense, and myrrh.

Matthew 2:10-11